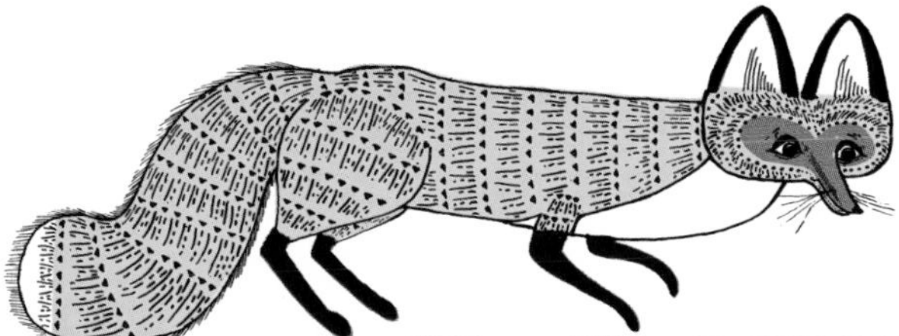

ROSIE'S WALK

Pat Hutchins

ROSIE'S WALK

ALADDIN PAPERBACKS

Aladdin Paperbacks
An imprint of Simon & Schuster
Children's Publishing Division
1230 Avenue of the Americas
New York, NY 10020

First Aladdin Paperbacks Edition, 1986

Rosie's Walk is published in a hardcover edition by Simon & Schuster Children's Publishing Division.

Printed and bound in the United States of America

27 29 30 28 26

Library of Congress catalog card number: 68-12090

ISBN 0-02-043750-1

For
Wendy
and
Stephen

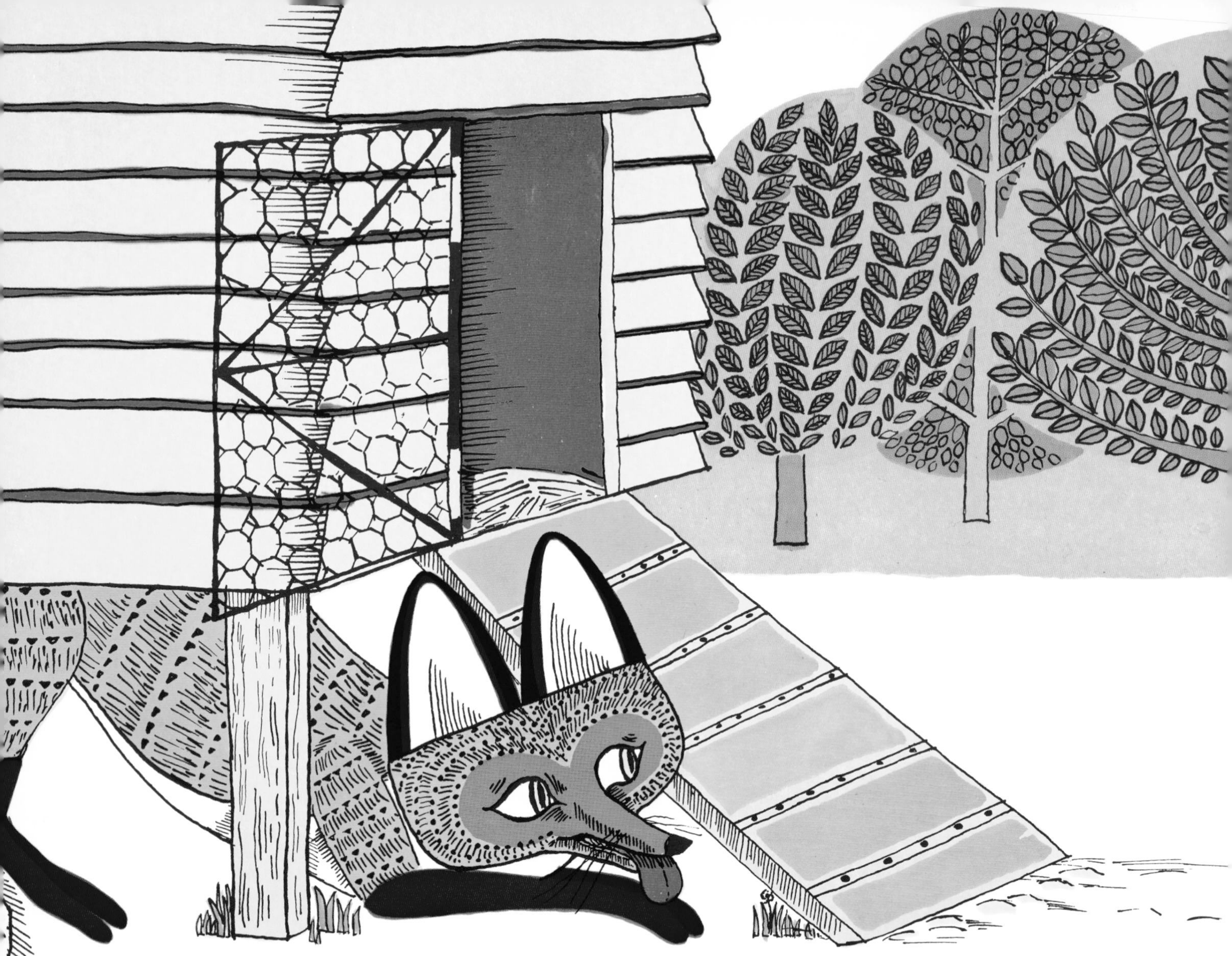

Rosie the hen went for a walk

across the yard

around

the

pond

over the haystack

past the mill

FLOUR

FLOUR

CORN
CORN
CORN

through the fence

under the beehives

and
got back
in time
for dinner.